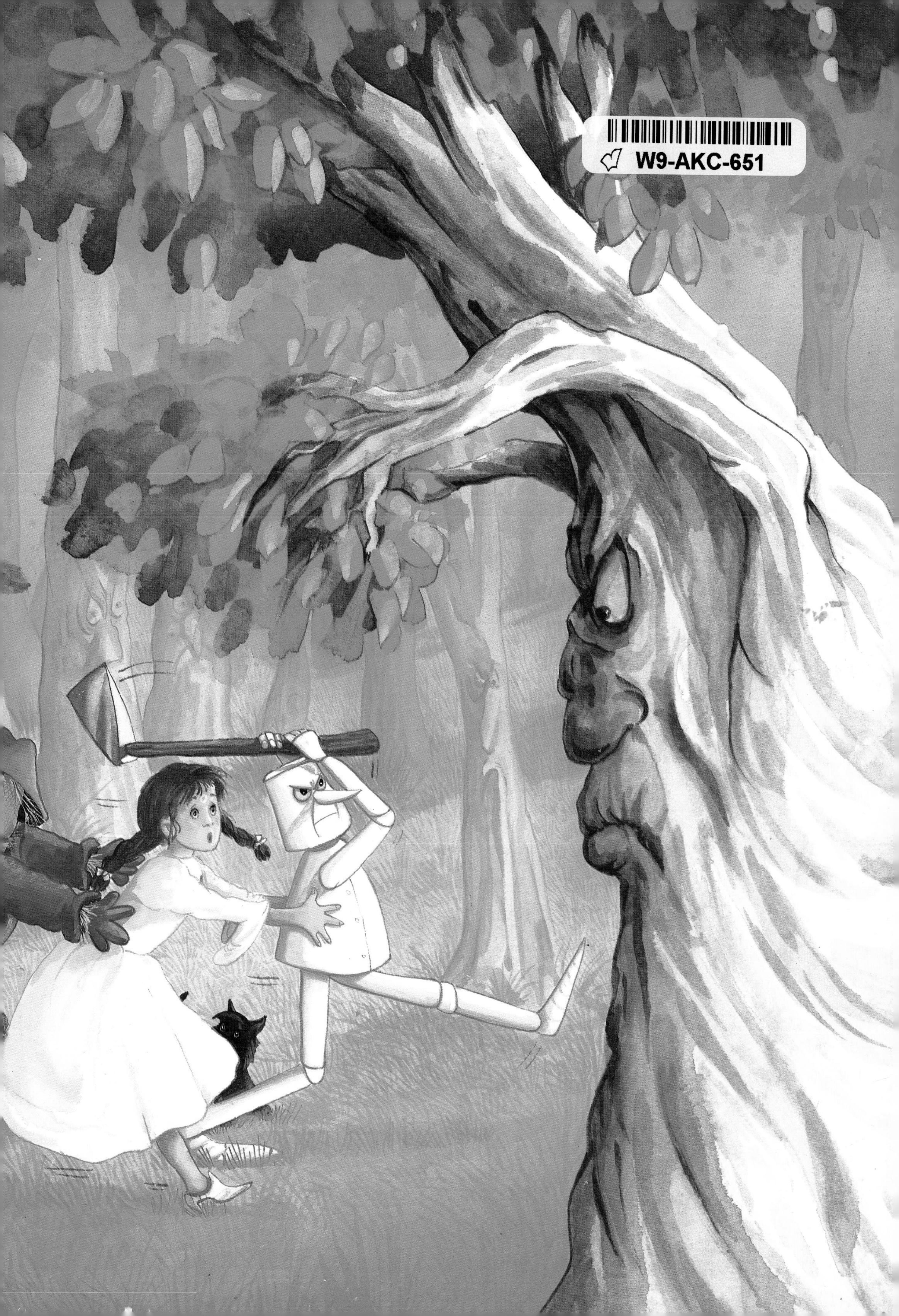

ISBN 1 85854 644 3
© Brimax Books Ltd 1997. All rights reserved.
Published by Brimax Books Ltd, Newmarket,
England, CB8 7AU 1997.
Printed in China.

The WIZARD of Oz

By L. Frank Baum

Adapted by Lucy Kincaid

Illustrated by Gill Guile

BRIMAX · NEWMARKET · ENGLAND

The Wizard of Oz

A cyclone carries Dorothy to the wonderful Land of Oz. There she meets the Scarecrow, the Tin Woodman, and the Lion. Together they follow the yellow brick road to the Emerald City. Each one of them has something special to ask the Wizard of Oz. Will he grant their wishes?

Contents

Dorothy lived with her Uncle Henry and Aunt Em in a little house on the great Kansas plain.

One day Uncle Henry looked up at the sky and said, "There's a cyclone coming, Em!"

"Quick, Dorothy!" called Aunt Em. "Run to the cellar. We'll be safe from the storm in there."

But before Dorothy could get to the cellar, the wind whirled the house around and lifted it into the sky. Dorothy and her dog, Toto, were trapped inside.

After a while, Dorothy and Toto fell asleep. When they woke up, they found themselves in a strange land.

"Welcome," said an old woman. "We want to thank you for killing the Wicked Witch of the East and for freeing our people."

"I haven't killed anyone," said Dorothy.

The old woman, who was the Good Witch of the North, pointed to two silver shoes sticking out from under the house. "Your house fell on the Wicked Witch and killed her," she said. Then the Good Witch gave the shoes to Dorothy to wear.

"Aunt Em will be worrying about me," said Dorothy. "Can you help me find my way home?"

"You must follow the yellow brick road to the Emerald City," said the Witch. "There you must ask the Wizard of Oz to help you." Then she kissed Dorothy on her forehead and disappeared.

Dorothy put on the silver shoes. She took some bread from the house and put it in a basket. With Toto beside her, she set off along the yellow brick road.

Dorothy Meets the Scarecrow

Dorothy was resting by a cornfield when she saw a Scarecrow wink at her.

"Hello," said the Scarecrow. "It's so boring here. If you could lift me down, I would be very grateful."

Dorothy easily lifted the Scarecrow from his pole.

"My name is Dorothy," she said to him. "I'm on my way to the Emerald City to see the Wizard of Oz. I'm going to ask him to help me find my way home."

"Do you think the Great Oz could give me a brain?" asked the Scarecrow.

"Come with me and ask him," said Dorothy.

At noon Dorothy sat down and took some bread from her basket.

"I'm glad I don't get hungry," said the Scarecrow. "My mouth is only painted. If I cut a hole in it to eat, my straw would come out."

Towards evening Dorothy, Toto and the Scarecrow came to a forest. The yellow brick road led them through it until they came to a cottage. Here they spent the night.

The next morning, Dorothy had just finished washing in the stream when she heard a deep groan. Standing amongst the trees was a man made entirely of tin. He was standing absolutely still. It seemed as if he couldn't move even if he wanted to.

"Was that you groaning?" asked Dorothy.

"Yes," said the Tin Woodman. "I've been groaning for a year, but no one has ever heard me. Please oil my joints. They are rusted and I cannot move. The oil can is in the cottage."

Dorothy oiled the Tin Woodman's joints.

"I could have stood there forever if you hadn't come along," said the Tin Woodman to Dorothy as he lowered his axe. "How did you happen to come this way?"

"The Scarecrow and I are on our way to the Emerald City to see the Wizard of Oz," said Dorothy. "I am going to ask him to help me get home, and the Scarecrow is going to ask him for a brain."

"Do you think the Great Oz could give me a heart?" asked the Tin Woodman.

"If he can give me a brain, I'm sure he could help you," said the Scarecrow.

"Why don't you come with us and ask him?" said Dorothy.

The Cowardly Lion

Dorothy, Toto, the Scarecrow and the Tin Woodman set off merrily along the yellow brick road.

After a while they heard a terrible roar, and a Lion leapt onto the road in front of them. He knocked the Scarecrow off his feet and scratched the Tin Woodman with his sharp claws.

Toto wasn't afraid of anyone. Barking loudly he ran towards the Lion. As the Lion opened his mouth to bite Toto, Dorothy hit the Lion hard on his nose.

"Don't you dare!" she shouted.

"But I didn't," said the Lion, rubbing his nose.

"No," said Dorothy. "But you tried. Only a coward would bite a little dog like Toto."

The Lion hung his head in shame.

"Why are you a coward?" asked Dorothy.

"I don't know," said the Lion. "I roar and make a lot of noise, but I'm easily frightened."

Dorothy told the Lion that they were going to the Emerald City to get help from the Great Oz.

"Do you think the Great Oz would give me some courage?" asked the Lion.

"Just as easily as he could give me a brain," said the Scarecrow.

"And me a heart," said the Tin Woodman.

"Or send me back to Kansas," said Dorothy.

"Then, if I may, I would like to come with you," said the Lion.

Before long they came to a ditch filled with jagged rocks. There was no way to cross it.

"I think I could jump over it," said the Lion. And although he was afraid of falling, he carried his new friends over the ditch one by one.

Later they came to another ditch. The Tin Woodman cut down a tree to make a bridge. Suddenly they heard the Kalidahs coming after them. The Kalidahs had the bodies of bears with heads like tigers. They were very fierce.

Dorothy and her friends crossed the bridge. Then the Tin Woodman swung his axe and cut through the bridge. The Kalidahs fell onto the rocks.

The River and the Poppy Field

That afternoon they came to a river. The Tin Woodman built a raft. They all climbed aboard.

The raft was halfway across the river when it was caught by the current. The Scarecrow pushed a pole into the mud to stop the raft. But before he could pull the pole out, the raft with all his friends was swept away. He was left clinging to the pole in the middle of the river.

The others could hear the Scarecrow calling goodbye as the raft was swept further and further away. There was nothing they could do to help him. They also had a problem of their own to solve. They had to get ashore.

The Lion leapt into the water, and with the Tin Woodman holding onto his tail and Dorothy pushing with a pole, the Lion managed to pull the raft ashore.

It was a long walk back to the yellow brick road.

"Look!" cried the Tin Woodman suddenly.

There was the Scarecrow, still clinging to the pole in the middle of the river.

"How can we rescue him?" asked Dorothy.

"I would do it for you if he wasn't so big and heavy," said a passing stork.

"He isn't heavy," said Dorothy. "He is stuffed with straw."

"That's alright then," said the stork. He picked the Scarecrow up by his arm and carried him back to his friends. Once again, they all set out for the Emerald City.

The yellow brick road led to a field of bright red poppies. The poppies had a powerful scent which could make people sleep forever if they stayed in the field. Dorothy did not know this. When she began to feel tired, she sat down. Soon Dorothy and Toto were both fast asleep.

"What shall we do?" asked the Tin Woodman.

"If we leave them here they will die," said the Lion. He was nearly asleep too.

"Run from this field," the Scarecrow told the Lion. "If you fall asleep, you will be too heavy to lift."

So the Lion bounded away before he fell asleep.

The Scarecrow and the Tin Woodman carried Dorothy and Toto. But they soon came across the Lion, fast asleep in the poppies. Knowing that they could not lift the Lion, they moved on and carried Dorothy and Toto out of the poppy field.

While they waited for Dorothy to wake up, the Tin Woodman saved a mouse from a wildcat. The mouse was Queen of the field mice.

"You have saved my life," she said. "What can my subjects do to help you?"

"They can help us rescue our friend, the Lion," said the Scarecrow. "He is asleep in the poppy field."

"Tell us what to do," said the Queen Mouse.

By the time Dorothy awoke, everything was ready. The Tin Woodman had made a truck, and each field mouse was carrying a long piece of string.

They went into the field and pushed and pulled the Lion until he was on the truck. They worked quickly, in case they fell asleep too. Then each mouse tied his piece of string to the truck. With the mice pulling and everyone else pushing, it didn't take very long to pull the lion to safety.

The Emerald City

As soon as the Lion was awake, they found their way back to the yellow brick road.

They stayed the night in a cottage. The next day they set off once more. Soon they noticed a green glow in the sky.

"That must be the Emerald City," said Dorothy.

By the afternoon they had reached a high, green wall and a gate studded with emeralds.

Dorothy rang the bell. The gate swung open. Before them stood a little, green man.

"I am the guard of the gate," he said.

He gave each of them a pair of spectacles to wear and then put on a pair himself. Dorothy and her friends followed the man through another gate into the Emerald City.

The Emerald City was a wonderful place. Everything in it was green - even the sky. In the middle of the city was the Palace of Oz.

Guarding the Palace was a soldier with green whiskers. He said Oz would see the friends one at a time. They would have to stay in the Palace for several days.

Dorothy was taken to see Oz first. Before she was allowed to see him, she had to put on a green dress. A green ribbon was tied around Toto's neck. Then they were taken to the Throne Room.

On the Throne sat an enormous head without a body, arms or legs.

"I am Oz, the Great and Terrible," said the head. "Who are you and what do you want?"

Dorothy said that she wanted to go home to Kansas.

"Where did you get those silver shoes?" asked Oz.

"My house fell on the Wicked Witch of the East and killed her," said Dorothy.

"Before I help you go home, you must do something for me," said the Wizard. "You must kill the Wicked Witch of the West."

"Even if I wanted to, I wouldn't know how to," said Dorothy.

"That is my answer," said Oz. "Only when you come back and tell me that she is dead will I send you back to Kansas."

The next morning it was the Scarecrow's turn to go into the Throne Room.

Oz appeared as a lady and said, "Kill the Wicked Witch of the West and I will give you a brain."

The morning after that it was the Tin Woodman's turn. Oz took the form of a dreadful looking beast.

"Kill the Wicked Witch of the West and I will give you a heart," said Oz.

Finally it was the Lion's turn. Oz appeared as a great ball of fire and said, "Kill the Wicked Witch of the West and I will give you courage."

Dorothy and her friends had no choice but to find the Wicked Witch of the West and kill her.

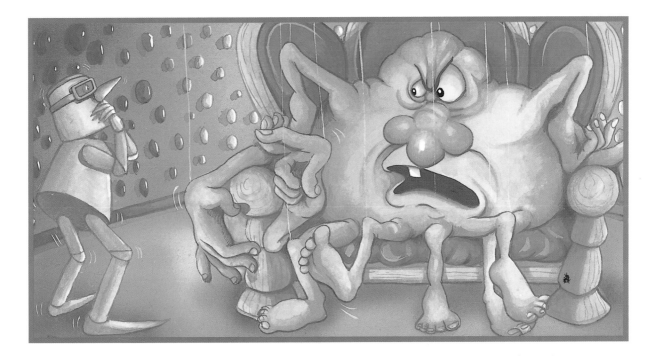

The Search for the Wicked Witch

The next day, they all headed West for the land of the Winkies, who were slaves of the Wicked Witch.

The Witch had only one eye, but it could see everywhere. She saw Dorothy and her friends.

The Witch sent a pack of wolves to kill them all. But the Tin Woodman killed the wolves with his axe.

The Witch sent a flock of crows to peck them to pieces. But the Scarecrow soon got rid of them.

The Witch was very angry. She called for a swarm of bees to sting Dorothy and her friends to death.

"Take out my straw and hide Dorothy, Toto and the Lion under it," said the Scarecrow to the Tin Woodman when he saw the bees coming.

The bee stings could not hurt the Tin Woodman. When the bees had gone, Dorothy put the straw back into the Scarecrow.

The Wicked Witch was getting more and more angry. Nothing was going right for her. She sent for the Winkies and gave them spears.

"Kill the strangers," she ordered them.

But when the Winkies found Dorothy and her friends, the Lion roared at them and they ran away.

The Witch put on her Golden Cap and called for the Winged Monkeys. They would have to obey her command.

The Rescue

The Witch said the magic words, "Ep-pe, pep-pe, kak-ke."

The Winged Monkeys appeared above Dorothy and her friends. They dropped the Tin Woodman onto some rocks and pulled all the straw from the Scarecrow. They took Dorothy, Toto and the Lion to the Wicked Witch's castle.

When the Witch saw Dorothy's silver shoes, she wanted them for herself. She tricked Dorothy into losing one.

"Give me back my shoe!" shouted Dorothy. She picked up a bucket filled with water and threw it over the Witch.

The Witch screamed and began to melt until she was nothing but a shapeless mess on the floor.

Dorothy, Toto and the Lion were free!

Now that the Wicked Witch was dead, the Winkies were happy to help Dorothy and the Lion. They hammered and polished the Tin Woodman until he was as good as new.

"If only the Scarecrow was here," said the Lion.

The Scarecrow's clothes were still in the tree where the Winged Monkeys had left them. The Tin Woodman cut down the tree, and they carried the clothes back to the castle. The Winkies helped to stuff them with straw, and soon the Scarecrow was as good as new.

"Now that the Witch is dead, we must go back to the Wizard of Oz and make him keep his promises," said Dorothy. "We'll ask the Queen of the Mice how to get there."

Dorothy blew on a whistle the Queen had given her when she was rescued from the poppy field. The Queen appeared.

"The Golden Cap is now yours," said the Queen. "You have three wishes. The Winged Monkeys will take you back to the Emerald City."

Dorothy put on the cap and called for the Winged Monkeys.

"What is your wish?" asked the King of the Monkeys.

"To go to the Emerald City," said Dorothy.

The Discovery of Oz

At the Emerald City, Dorothy and her friends were taken to the Throne Room.

A voice asked, "Is the Wicked Witch dead?"

"Yes," said Dorothy. "Now you must keep your promises to us."

"Come back tomorrow," said the voice.

The Lion gave an angry roar. A screen in the corner of the room fell with a crash. Behind it was an old man with a bald head and a wrinkled face.

"Who are you?" asked the Tin Woodman.

"I am Oz, the Great and Terrible," said the little man.

"You're a humbug," said the Scarecrow.

"Does anyone else know you're a humbug?" asked Dorothy.

"No one," said the man. "The Wicked Witches would have destroyed me if they had found out."

"How will I get my brain?" asked the Scarecrow.

"How will I get my heart?" asked the Tin Woodman.

"How will I get my courage?" asked the Lion.

"And how will I get home?" asked Dorothy.

"Come back tomorrow," said Oz. "I will see what I can do to help you."

"How will I get back to Kansas?" asked Dorothy.

"That might take longer to work out," said Oz.

The Wizard's Magic Art

The next day they returned to the Throne Room.

Oz made the Scarecrow a brain with pins and needles. He made the Tin Woodman a heart with silk and sawdust. He gave the Lion a drink from a green bottle that filled him with courage.

Oz was very pleased with himself.

"I will make a balloon to take Dorothy home," said Oz. "Then I will go with her. I'm tired of being shut up in these rooms and of being afraid people will discover I'm not really a wizard."

When the balloon was ready, the Tin Woodman chopped some wood and made a fire to fill the balloon with hot air.

As Oz climbed into the basket, he told the people that the Scarecrow would be the ruler of the Emerald City.

Dorothy ran towards the balloon with Toto in her arms.

"Hurry, Dorothy," called Oz, who was already inside the basket.

But Dorothy wasn't quick enough. The balloon began to rise into the air without her.

"Come back!" screamed Dorothy.

"I can't," called Oz, floating higher and higher into the sky. "Goodbye!"

And that was the last they ever saw of the wonderful Wizard of Oz.

Dorothy sat and cried.

The Scarecrow had his brain and was proud to be the new ruler of the Emerald City.

The Tin Woodman had his heart and the Lion had his courage.

Everyone was happy except for Dorothy.

Journey to the South

"Call the Winged Monkeys and ask them to carry you home over the desert," said the Scarecrow to Dorothy.

But the Winged Monkeys were unable to help. Finally she was told to go and ask Glinda, the Good Witch of the South, to help her.

Once again the friends left the Emerald City and set off for the South, led by the Scarecrow.

They were about to go into a forest when the branches of a large tree wrapped themselves around the Scarecrow. The same thing happened to the Tin Woodman when he tried to pass. But he chopped at the tree with his axe. The tree let the Scarecrow go and let the Tin Woodman pass by safely.

"Quickly," the Tin Woodman cried to the others, and they all passed safely.

After that there was no more trouble and they walked on through the forest until nightfall.

The next morning they came to a clearing in the forest where hundreds of animals were gathered.

Dorothy was frightened by all the growling.

"There is nothing to be afraid of," said the Lion. "They are holding a meeting."

When the animals saw the Lion, they became silent. The biggest tiger came forward and bowed to the Lion.

"Welcome King of the Beasts," said the tiger. "You have come just in time to save us from our enemy."

The tiger told the Lion that a great spider had come into the forest. It was seizing the animals and eating them.

"If I destroy your enemy, will you obey me as your King?" asked the Lion.

"We will!" roared all the animals.

The Lion killed the giant spider, and all the animals bowed before him.

"I will return to rule over you when Dorothy is safely on her way home," said the Lion.

Dorothy gets her Wish

They continued on their way. Soon they came to the bottom of a steep, rocky hill.

"Keep away!" said a voice. "This hill belongs to us."

A strange creature stepped out from behind a rock. It was very short, it had no arms and its head was flat on top.

"We must go on," said the Scarecrow.

Suddenly the creature stretched its neck right out from its body and hit the Scarecrow with its flat head. Many more of the creatures appeared.

"What shall we do?" asked Dorothy.

"Call the Winged Monkeys," said the Tin Woodman.

For the last time, Dorothy summoned the Winged Monkeys. They appeared within minutes. They carried Dorothy and her friends over the hill and into the land of the Quadlings, where the Good Witch of the South lived.

They found the Good Witch sitting on her throne of rubies in her castle.

"I will tell you how to get back to Kansas," she said to Dorothy. "But you must give me the Golden Cap. I will command the Winged Monkeys to take the Scarecrow back to the Emerald City and the Lion to the forest. I will send the Tin Woodman to rule in the land of the Winkies."

Dorothy was pleased for her friends.

"The silver shoes will take you home," said Glinda. "You could have gone back to Kansas the very first day you arrived here."

"But then I wouldn't have my brain," said the Scarecrow.

"Or I my heart," said the Tin Woodman.

"Or I my courage," said the Lion.

"That is true," said Dorothy. "But now if you don't mind, I would really like to go home."

"You must knock your heels together three times," said Glinda, "and command the shoes to take you home."

Dorothy took Toto in her arms and kissed her friends goodbye. Then she knocked her heels together three times.

"Take me home to Aunt Em," she said.

Suddenly she was whirling through the air. Then, just as suddenly, she stopped whirling and was rolling on the grass. There in front of her was the new house Uncle Henry had built after the cyclone. And there was Aunt Em.

"Where in the world did you come from?" asked Aunt Em as she took Dorothy into her arms and kissed her.

"From the wonderful Land of Oz," said Dorothy. "But oh, Aunt Em, I'm so glad to be home again."